Elmo's Mother Goose Rhymes

By Constance Allen
Illustrated by Maggie Swanson

 A GOLDEN BOOK · NEW YORK

Visit us on the Web!
randomhousekids.com
SesameStreetBooks.com
www.sesamestreet.org
Educators and librarians, for a variety of teaching tools, visit us at RHTeachersLibrarians.com
ISBN: 978-1-101-93994-9
Printed in the United States of America
10 9 8 7 6

Little Bo-Peep was counting sheep,
But forgot what comes after ten.
The Count cried, "It's clear! Eleven, my dear!
And now let us count them again!"

Pat-a-cake, pat-a-cake, baker's man.
Make lots of cakes as fast as you can.
Mix them and pour them
And bake them till they're through.
Then GOBBLE them up!
Pan delicious, too!

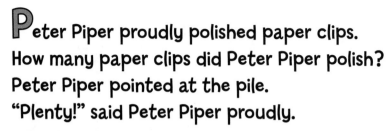

Peter Piper proudly polished paper clips.
How many paper clips did Peter Piper polish?
Peter Piper pointed at the pile.
"Plenty!" said Peter Piper proudly.

Little Jack Horner sat in a corner,
Eating his anchovy pie.
A bird came to play,
Jack yelled, "Go away!"
And said, "What a good grouch am I!"

Little Miss Muffet sat on her tuffet,
Eating a bowl of stew.
When a very big spider
Sat down right beside her,
She said, "There is plenty for you!"

Hickory, dickory, dock.
The bird climbed up the clock!
When the clock struck two,
He cried, "CUCK-OO!
I'm the loudest clock on the block!"

Old King Cole was a merry old soul,
For he ate only healthy food.
He called for his bread,
And he called for his cheese,
And he called for his fruit, nicely stewed.

Jack be nimble,
Jack be fast.
Jack is first,
And I am last.

Hey, diddle, diddle,
The Twiddlebugs fiddle,
And Gladys moos at the moon.
Barkley barks to see such sport,
And the grouch bangs his can with a spoon!

Sing a song of sixes,
Six monsters do a dance,
Six monsters with suspenders
Holding up their pants.

Look above their heads
And count what you see there.
Six extremely silly hats!
Now, what a thing to wear!

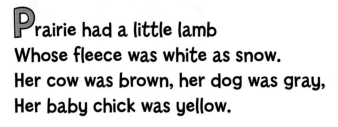

Prairie had a little lamb
Whose fleece was white as snow.
Her cow was brown, her dog was gray,
Her baby chick was yellow.

One friend had shaggy purple fur,
The other friend was blue,
And everywhere the three friends went,
The pets would follow, too!

Twinkle, twinkle, little star,
Elmo wonders what you are.
Far away, up in the sky,
Glinting like a firefly.
Twinkle, twinkle, in the air,
Elmo waves at you up there.